A FROG and DOG book

P9-CLB-109

# Hog on a Log

by Janee Trasler

**ACORN**™
SCHOLASTIC INC.

# For superstar, Nicole.

Library of Congress Cataloging-in-Publication Data

Names: Trasler, Janee, author, illustrator. Title: Hog on a log / by Janee Trasler.
Description: First edition. | New York : Acorn/Scholastic Inc., 2020. |
Series: A Frog and Dog book ; 3 | Audience: Ages 4-6. | Audience: Grades K-1. | Summary: "Told in rhyming text, Dog and Frogs are enjoying riding a log in the pond, but then Hog comes along and is not willing to share the log, or the lunch Dog has made. Hog wants it all, so Dog and Frogs need to teach Hog a lesson about friendship and sharing"-- Provided by publisher. Identifiers: LCCN 2020001678 (print) | LCCN 2020001679 (ebook) | ISBN 9781338540499 (library binding) | ISBN 9781338540475 (paperback) | ISBN 9781338540505 (ebook) Subjects: LCSH: Frogs—Juvenile fiction. | Dogs—Juvenile fiction. | Swine—Juvenile fiction. | Sharing—Juvenile fiction. | Friendship--Juvenile fiction. | Stories in rhyme. | CYAC: Stories in rhyme. | Frogs—Fiction. | Dogs—Fiction. | Pigs—Fiction. | Sharing—Fiction. | Friendship--Fiction. | LCGFT: Stories in rhyme.
Classification: LCC PZ8.3.T688 Ho 2020 (print) | LCC PZ8.3.T688 (ebook) | DDC (E)--dc23
LC record available at https://lccn.loc.gov/2020001678
LC ebook record available at https://lccn.loc.gov/2020001679

10 9 8 7 6 5 4 3 2 1          20 21 22 23 24

Printed in China          62

First edition, October 2020

Edited by Rachel Matson

Book design by Christian Zelaya

What does Dog see?

CRACK

CRASH

SPLASH

Dog on a log.

One frog and a dog on a log.

Two frogs and a dog on a log.

Three frogs and a dog on a log.

Here comes a hog.

Hi, Hog.

Hog on a log.

# Dog makes a bun.

Hog takes the bun.

Dog makes a cake.

23

Hog takes the cake.

# Dog cooks peas.

Munch

Munch

Munch

Dog wants to eat too.

# What can Frog do?

# Hog takes the pie.

# What can Dog do?

41

Three frogs,
one dog, and
a hog on a log.

# About the Author

**Janee Trasler** loves to make kids laugh. Whether she is writing books, drawing pictures, singing songs, or performing with her puppets, she is going for the giggle. Janee lives in Texas with her hubby, her doggies, and one very squeaky guinea pig.

# YOU CAN DRAW HOG!

**1** Draw a circle.

**2** Draw two more circles for the eyes. Add two dots.

**3** Add two sideways hearts for the ears.

**4** Draw an oval for the nose. Add two dots in the middle.

**5** Add a half-circle for the mouth.

**6** Color in your drawing!

## WHAT'S YOUR STORY?

Dog makes a bun for lunch.
Imagine **you** are having lunch with Dog.
What other foods would you like to eat?
Write and draw your story!